Publisher's Note

This book is an introduction to just a few of the amazing variety of rich and wondrous stories the different peoples of the world have told to make sense of the world around them and to approach the big questions about the Universe.

Sometimes different cultures can have very similar myths and stories exist in many different versions and tellings. Some stories may be familiar to you and others less so. Many have played a part in shaping people's view of the world. Some are sacred beliefs that are respected and cherished to this day.

Mythical Science explores a few threads of the rich and colourful tapestry of the world's complex mythologies and beliefs. The creators of this book have had to make difficult choices about what to include and what to leave out. But hopefully this is just the start of your journey and the book will inspire you to want to find out more.

For Justin. R.L-O.

First published in Great Britain 2022 by Red Shed, part of Farshore

An imprint of HarperCollins*Publishers*
1 London Bridge Street, London SE1 9GF
www.farshore.co.uk

HarperCollins*Publishers*
1st Floor, Watermarque Building, Ringsend Road, Dublin 4, Ireland

Text copyright © Rebecca Lewis-Oakes 2022
Illustrations copyright © HarperCollins*Publishers* Limited 2022
Rebecca Lewis-Oakes has asserted her moral rights.

ISBN 978 0 7555 0114 4
Printed in Italy.
001

Consultancy by Dr Mike Goldsmith and Dr Stephen P. Kershaw.

A CIP catalogue record for this title is available from the British Library.

Stay safe online. Any website addresses listed in this book are correct at the time of going to print. However, Farshore is not responsible for content hosted by third parties. Please be aware that online content can be subject to change and websites can contain content that is unsuitable for children. We advise that all children are supervised when using the internet.

MIX
Paper from
responsible sources
FSC
www.fsc.org
FSC™ C007454

MYTHICAL SCIENCE

Rebecca Lewis-Oakes

Illustrated by Max Rambaldi

RED SHED

Our Earth

Do you ever look up at the sky, or at the world around you, and wonder how it all got there? Congratulations, that makes you a human! Since the beginning of time, people have always asked BIG questions about our planet. Today, science helps us to figure out the answers. But before we could measure how big the Earth is (40,075km around the middle, since you asked), or identify teeny tiny atoms too small for the eye to see, how did people explain the world and answer these big questions?

How does the sky stay up?

Ancient people didn't have telescopes. Microscopes hadn't been invented. They didn't know how far away the Moon was, or what caused thunder and lightning. So they explained the world through magical stories called myths. These stories were passed down from generation to generation and some people still have them as the basis of their beliefs today.

Where do rainbows come from?

Sometimes different cultures can have very similar myths. Often, there are several versions of the same story told. Early ancient Greeks thought that planet Earth must be a mother goddess, Gaia, since it gives us life. (And people still talk about Mother Nature today.) But the ancient Greeks also started to use the power of science to explain and understand the world. People saw that there were scientific explanations to things happening around them, as well as their different sacred tales.

How did the Moon get there?

Why does the Sun rise?

Now you can look things up to find out what scientists have figured out all about our planet. Sometimes you can create your own experiments to find the awesome answers. But the myths are still amazing stories — and you can enjoy them while understanding the science too! So turn the page and get stuck in to some magical myths and sensational science about our incredible planet.

What Shape is the World?

Welcome to planet Earth! Did you know, many ancient peoples used to think the world was flat? Well, if you couldn't fly above Earth in a plane or spaceship, you might not know there was anything beyond the horizon. All kinds of magical myths grew up around the shape of our world and Universe.

The seas were said to run over the edge of the world in ancient Egyptian myths. They flowed into a watery underworld.

This tree-mendous myth said that the world was a ginormous tree! Yes, Slavic stories told of gods living in the upper branches and humans in the middle

The Aztec Universe was made up of four quarters of our human world, nine underworlds and THIRTEEN layers of sky worlds.

An ancient Indian myth had the world resting on giant elephants, who were themselves standing on the back of a giant tortoise or turtle.

Sensational science

Now we know that Earth is not a giant turtle or tree, and it's not even flat with an edge to fall off. There is no edge! We know that the Earth is (almost) a sphere – we've seen it from outer space to prove it! Scientists have shown that Earth is the third of eight planets in our Solar System – that means HUGE things orbiting (travelling round) the Sun, our closest star. Some planets are made mainly of gas but the Earth is made of rock and metal. Extra-specially, Earth has liquid water on it, which gives life to everything on our planet. Hooray!

Why does the Sun rise?

The Sun rising and setting every day is so important that many ancient people told incredible tales about why it happens.

The Aztec Sun god, Huitzilopochtli, was born already at war with his brothers and sisters, the stars. He chased them and they scattered all over the sky. The Aztecs said that the Sun chased away the stars every morning.

The Babylonian sun god Shamash emerged from the Sun's Gate in the mountain of the horizon every morning at sunrise. He travelled across the sky and entered the Underworld every evening at sunset.

The Menominee nation and some other native American peoples tell of Rabbit and Owl arguing over how much light there should be in the world. Who won? They tied. They agreed to let the Sun shine brightly in the day for Rabbit and the Moon shine less brightly at night to be darker for Owl.

Sensational science

Um, actually, the Sun doesn't rise and set! Earth rotates (turns around) completely once every day. To us, it looks like the Sun rises in the east, moves across the sky and then sets in the west. But really, the Sun is staying still and WE are spinning round, facing the Sun by day and turning away from it as night falls. But we don't feel the movement because we're moving with Earth!

Think about when you're on a roundabout – wheeee! The other things in the playground look like they're whizzing past you. But you know that, really, they are staying still and you only see them once every rotation of the roundabout. The Sun rising and setting is the same idea!

Why is the Moon up in the sky?

As the Sun sets, the Moon rises. Ancient people watched and wondered why this was, and they also questioned how the Moon got up into the sky in the first place. Several myths have Sun and Moon gods chasing each other across the sky, while others tell of giant eggs, or stars feeding the Moon.

A Malawian myth says that the morning star starved the Moon in the day, and the evening star fed it at night. The Xhosa people tell a story of a new, full Moon that pops out of the sea each month, then slowly gets smaller and faded away.

The Moon was an actual goddess to the ancient Greeks. She was called Selene and drove two winged horses across the night sky.

But Hindu tradition said the Moon was a god, Chandra. He also drove a chariot but his was pulled either by lots of white horses or by antelopes!

One egg-citing Chinese myth said that the giant Pangu hatched from a cosmic egg at the beginning of time – crack! A piece of the eggshell became the Moon.

Sensational science

Before scientists could carry out experiments on the Moon, they made up stories about how the Moon got to be in the sky too! They just used scientific language, rather than gods and monsters, and used measurements and mathematics, not just imagination. Scientists thought maybe the Moon was a passing asteroid that got caught in Earth's gravity, or that Earth was once spinning so fast that a bit broke off, which became the Moon. It wasn't until 1969, when American astronauts landed on the Moon, that they could do experiments to figure out what the Moon was made of and maybe how it got there.

So, how DID the Moon come to be where it is? Now, most scientists agree that, at some point, billions of years ago, a young Earth and another planet crashed into each other. This giant crash broke the other planet up – and some of it became the Moon. And it stays where it is, travelling around Earth because Earth's gravity keeps it in our orbit.

How does the sky stay up?

Look up. Now look down. Why is the ground under our feet and the sky above our heads? Why is it not the other way round? Great question!

Ancient people explained this with myths about strong gods or heroes holding up the sky. They each had this job for all eternity . . . they must have been pretty tired!

Probably the most comfortable sky-holding god was Polynesian Tāne, a forest god. He lay on his back to push up the sky god Rangi with his legs, away from the Earth goddess Papa.

Here's something interesting . . . very few ancient cultures had a word for blue! Did they not see the sky as blue or did they just not know what to call that colour? We'll never know . . .

Then there was the Greek Titan, Atlas. After a battle, the god Zeus forced Atlas to hold the heavens on his shoulders forever. Ouch.

Egyptian Shu, god of air, however, stood holding up sky goddess Nut, away from earth god Geb. It allowed life on Earth to flourish, but his arms must have ached!

Sensational science

Do these giant beings really hold up the sky? Well science now tells us that it's all about gravity. Earth, like most planets, is surrounded by a blanket of gases – air – called the atmosphere. This blanket is held in place by Earth's gravity. Gravity is a force that attracts everything to everything else. It keeps the Moon in its orbit and it pulls you back down to Earth when you jump up high.

The sky is the atmosphere as we look up at it from Earth. So really, the answer to the question is not how the sky stays up, but how gravity pulls it down!

Where do rainbows come from?

Rainbows are one of the most magical things to see in nature. Each one is a shimmering curve in the sky, with bright bands of different colours.

Several ancient peoples believed that rainbows were a bridge between Earth and heaven, or wherever they believed the gods lived.

The god Izanagi and goddess Izanami slid down their rainbow bridge from heaven one day and pulled up the islands of Japan with a spear!

The Māori god of rainbows, Uenuku, fell in love with a girl made of mist, and was turned into a rainbow so he could live with her in the sky.

Sensational science

But where do rainbows REALLY come from? Well, sunlight is a mixture of colours. The way our eyes work means that we see these mixed colours as white. When sunlight shines into a raindrop in the air, it splits up into its colours, filling the drop with coloured lights. These coloured lights bounce, or reflect, off the back of the raindrop and back out into the air. When millions of raindrops do this at the same time, we see the coloured light as a rainbow.

One Cherokee myth says that rainbows are the hem of the Sun's coat. That's some pretty fabulous heavenly fashion!

But ancient Greek goddess Iris spun rainbows with her feet as she flew through the air delivering messages to gods and mortals.

Ever found a pot of gold at the end of a rainbow? No, sadly that's just an ancient Irish myth. And there actually is no end to a rainbow – they're a perfect circle if you are high up enough in the sky to see! But from where we stand on the ground we see them as an arc.

Does the Sun ever disappear?

It does sometimes disappear in the daytime! Some ancient peoples were super worried about this. They thought it meant DOOM. They made up wonderful stories about it.

Quick, run! In Norse myths, sky wolves Skoll and Hati were said to chase and eat the Sun and Moon.

Sensational science

Don't worry, the Sun doesn't really get eaten. Sometimes the Moon gets between Earth and the Sun and blocks out all the Sun's light. This is called a total solar eclipse. It happens several times a year, but only on a very small part of Earth's surface, where the Moon's shadow falls, and in a different place each time. In any one place, centuries can pass between one solar eclipse and the next.

Scientists can now predict the exact day and time and the exact spot on Earth for seeing an eclipse, and it's a huge event.

Some amazing ancient people predicted solar eclipses! The Mayans had extremely accurate calendars around 2,000 years ago. They knew when to expect an eclipse – it saved them a lot of stress.

Ribbit! In ancient Vietnam, they explained eclipses by the myth of a giant toad eating the Sun. The toad's master, Lord Hahn, always managed to convince it to spit it back out, though – phew. The Sun was probably pretty hot to eat anyway.

What are shooting stars?

Ever wished upon a star? A shooting star? Ancient Europeans didn't wish on shooting stars – they thought they were a saint's tears. That's pretty sad for something so pretty in the night sky!

In East Africa, some ancient people thought shooting stars were gods and goddesses flitting across the heavens.

And Yolngu people in Australia believe a shooting star is a message from a dead person, showing relatives that they have arrived safely in the spirit land.

Sensational science

Now we know shooting stars are not really stars at all. They start off as meteoroids – chunks of space grit rushing through space. As soon as they enter Earth's atmosphere, they burn up and become meteors. The heat from the burning causes the 'shooting star' tail effect in the sky.

What are clouds?

Clouds are fluffy sheep sleeping in the sky. They're cotton wool that floated away. No, of course not! But ancient people had many myths about what they thought they were . . .

Ancient myths often say that clouds are houses for goddesses and gods. Zulu goddess Mbaba Mwana Waresa is said to live in the clouds, in a hut made of rainbow arches. She rules over the rain.

Christian angels are often pictured as living in the clouds, too, where they are high in the sky and closer to heaven.

And what about fog? Feth fiadha in Irish mythology was a supernatural fog that kept the magical folk invisible.

Sensational science

Now that planes and satellites can take us above the clouds to check, we can't see any gods living up there. Science tells us there are four main types of clouds, depending on how high they are in the sky and at what temperature.

When water, a liquid, gets hot, it evaporates and changes into an invisible gas called water vapour. Water vapour is all around us in the air. Warm air full of water vapour floats up, up, up into the sky. High up in the sky, the air is cold, and the water vapour gas cools down and collects into water droplets, which collect together to form clouds. When the water drops in a cloud are big and heavy enough, these heavy drops fall back down to Earth again as rain. That process is part of what is called the water cycle.

cirrus

cumulus

cumulonimbus

stratus

What's the difference between rain, hail and snow?

Wow, ancient weather gods got really specific! Myths tell us that rain, hail and snow are all caused by very different gods and goddesses in the clouds.

Albanian gods Shurdh and Verbt cause hailstorms.

Cailleach Bheur

Kuraokami

Khuno

Dodola is the Slavic goddess of rain. Whenever she milks her heavenly cows (which we call clouds), their milk falls as rain.

Snow is sent down by Cailleach Bheur in Scottish myth. In Japanese tradition, it is created by the god Kuraokami and the Incan people believed it was sent by the god Khuno.

cold air

warm air

Sensational science

Science now tells us that rain, hail and snow all start the same way . . . in clouds made up of raindrops. Whether they fall as rain, hail or snow depends on the temperature up in the cloud. Snow happens when it is freezing cold up in the clouds and tiny ice crystals stick together to form snowflakes. Hail happens when rising air inside clouds pushes raindrops up into cold air, and the drops freeze before falling.

What makes the wind blow?

If I told you that Aeolus, the Greek god of the winds, held the north, south, east and west winds in a bag, then let them out, would you believe me?

warm air

cold air

Sensational science

OK, the cat's out of the bag. The scientific explanation for wind is actually a difference in air pressure. You have to think big now, really big. No – even bigger than that. Think about the whole planet Earth . . .

When the weather is sunny, the sunlight heats the land (or the sea), and the air just above it warms up. It swells, and this makes it less dense (lighter). So, it rises. Cooler, denser air nearby flows in to take the place of the warm air, and this flowing air is the wind.

What are thunder and lightning?

Thunderbolt and lightning – very, very frightening? Or very very sensational science? Thunderstorms are so dramatic that many ancient peoples across the world thought they were caused by thunder gods hurling down weapons when they were angry. (Well, they'd hardly be sleeping gods making all that fuss, would they?)

The mighty Norse god Thor had a massive hammer called Mjolnir, which he would throw to send down lightning bolts and destroy anything that angered him.

Zeus was the ancient Greek god of the sky, thunder and lightning. He would throw a thunderbolt to zap his enemies. Or really anyone who made him cross. Look out!

Yoruba god Shango wields a powerful axe. With it, he can cast 'thunderstone' to Earth to anyone who offends him.

The supremely powerful Thunderbirds in several native American cultures didn't need a weapon. Their flapping wings caused thunder and flashing eyes caused lightning all by themselves.

These magical myths got it right that thunder and lightning are closely linked, and come from the same source. But it's not an angry god in a cloud, it's the science of static electricity and charged particles in the cloud causing the commotion.

Sensational science

In a cumulonimbus cloud (that's the really big one), when warm air rises it makes the watery and icy particles inside the cloud jumble up. They move about and rub against each other, causing static electricity. Eventually, the electric charge builds up – the top of the cloud is positive (+) and the bottom of the cloud is negative (–).

The negative charge gets so large that it is attracted to a high point on Earth. The attraction is strong enough that electricity flows suddenly to that point.

ZAP! LIGHTNING STRIKE!

The lightning is so hot that it makes a flash of light and forces air particles in its path to jump out of the way. This sudden extreme movement causes a burst of soundwaves:

KABOOM! The noise of THUNDER.

And Varja was the deadly lightning bolt held by Hindu god of thunder, Indra.

Do we always get the weather right?

Today's weather report is brought to you by the science of meteorology. That's a big word, and it means 'the study of things in the air'. Meteorologists have all kinds of tools to figure out what's going on up in the sky, so they can predict when it will rain, snow, sleet or just be gorgeously sunny.

In the ancient past, people tried to predict the weather – this was one of the oldest and longest-running science experiments ever! For example, from carefully observing clouds they knew that a great big cumulonimbus cloud meant a thunderstorm was on its way. High, wispy cirrus clouds usually meant fair weather was coming.

In ancient Babylon, officials kept notes on the weather every day for nearly 800 years. From this careful record-keeping, they were able to predict many weather events from patterns they had seen many times before.

Ancient Greek writers also made lots of weather observations. Hesoid said that when snails climbed up houses, it was time to harvest. According to Theophrastus, geese honking more than normal signalled a storm coming. And Plutarch claimed that crocodiles could predict the flooding of the Nile by where they laid their eggs.

Meteorologists today make careful observations and records, just like the ancients did. But scientists now have much more accurate instruments to make measurements, such as satellites, weather balloons and powerful computers. That means that weather predictions are more accurate. No one seems to consult the snails any more — a shame!

But they're not ALWAYS right. The weather still sometimes surprises us! There's still so much more to find out about our planet. There are plenty more stories to tell. Those myths and legends inspire beautiful beliefs about the Earth. And we can retell them ourselves, while we keep researching the sensational science behind the world's greatest stories.

Glossary

asteroid
A large rocky or metal body in space, orbiting the Sun

astronaut
A person who travels into space

atmosphere
A layer of gas or gases surrounding a planet

cloud
A group of very small floating drops of water or ice crystals in the sky

Earth
Our planet!

eclipse
When one object in the sky moves into the shadow of another object. For example, a solar eclipse is when the Moon's shadow crosses Earth's surface, sometimes completely blocking out the Sun from view!

electricity
The movement of tiny particles called electrons. This flow of energy can provide electrical power for machines. Static electricity is a build-up of electrical charge on a surface. 'Static' means 'staying in place' – the particles don't flow.

eternity
For ever – time with no beginning or end (whoa!)

experiment
A planned test to find out how an idea matches the real world

gas
One of the states of matter. Matter is made up of tiny particles. How close they are together changes how they look and behave.

god and goddess
A powerful spirit, more powerful than humans, that according to many myths controls what happens in the world. Different religions and cultures have different gods and goddesses.

gravity
A force that pulls objects down to Earth

horizon
If you look into the distance, the horizon is the line you can see between the ground (or sea) and the sky.

meteoroid
Piece of rock (much smaller than an asteroid) in space, orbiting the Sun. Meteors are meteoroids that enter Earth's atmosphere and burn up – also known as shooting stars!

meteorology
Scientific study of the weather

microscope
A scientific instrument that makes tiny things look bigger

Moon
A large rocky or icy ball orbiting another large object in space. Earth has a Moon, as do other planets in our Solar System.

myth
A traditional story to explain otherwise mysterious natural events or religious beliefs

orbit
The path an object takes around another object in space. Earth orbits the Sun by moving in a path around it once every roughly 365 days (= a year!).

particle
One of the teeny tiny pieces of matter that make up everything in our Universe

planet
A large object orbiting a star in space

Solar System
The Sun and everything that orbits the Sun in space. This includes Earth, the other planets, their moons and millions of asteroids and meteoroids.

sphere
A round ball shape

star
A huge, glowing ball of gas in the Universe. Our closest star is the Sun.

telescope
A scientific instrument to make faraway things seem closer

temperature
The measure of how hot or cold something is

Underworld
An imaginary world under the ground where spirits, gods or dead people's souls might live

Universe
EVERYTHING THAT EXISTS! Everything in our Solar System and beyond.

water cycle
The movement of water round and round between Earth and the sky. Water vapour floats up into the sky, collects into clouds, falls as rain, runs along and through the ground and into the sea, and floats up into the sky again.

water vapour
Water when it is in the form of gas. When water is heated, its particles spread apart and rise up to form vapour.

Cultures and peoples

This book mentions many different peoples and their amazing beliefs. They have all influenced our way of thinking to this very day. Some are still around, while others lived thousands of years ago. This is where they all came from:

Africa
Ancient Egyptians
Malawians
Xhosa
Yoruba
Zulu

Americas
Aztecs
Maya
Native North Americans
   including Cherokee
   and Menominee
Incas

Asia
Ancient Babylonians
Ancient Chinese
Ancient Indians (Hindus)
Ancient Japanese
Ancient Vietnamese

Australasia
Māori
Polynesians
Yolngu

Europe
Albanians
Ancient Greeks
Ancient Irish
Christian (medieval)
Norse
Ancient Scottish
Slavic